JINGLE BELL

Santa's Lost Puppy

by

Ashley N. Groves

To order additional copies of this book, contact:
Xlibris
1-888-795-4274
www.Xlibris.com
Orders@Xlibris.com

I would like to dedicate this book to all children who need a little Christmas fun and inspiration.

Have you ever heard of a dog named Jingle Bell? He is Santa's secret puppy and he has gone missing. Jingle Bell fell out of Santa's large gift bag on Christmas Eve near a little house. He is a little black puppy with white little spots, and the way to tell that it is definitely Jingle Bell is by the gold bell around his neck. Keep your eye out and if you see him, let Santa know.

In the cold wet woods, Jingle Bell wanders around looking for someone to help him. Jingle Bell notices a little baby deer.

"Hello," says Jingle Bell.
"Hey," replies the baby deer.
"Have you seen Santa?"
"No I haven't, are you lost?"
"Yes, I am Santa's puppy, and I can't find him anywhere, can you
help me find him?"
"Sure, this could be a great adventure."

Jingle Bell and his new friend Lucy, the baby deer, travel looking for someone else to help them. Scared, they wander farther and farther, hungry and lost. Next, they notice a little chubby white rabbit.

"Hey," says Jingle Bell and Lucy.
Scared, the bunny replies, "umm Hello?" as he is shaking out of his fur.
"What's your name?" they ask.
"Umm, my name is Molly."
"Hello Molly, nice to meet you. Have you seen Santa? I really need to find him."
"No I haven't, but I can help you look for him."

Jingle Bell, Lucy and now Molly keep venturing on until they find themselves stomping through several feet of snow.

"Where are we?" Molly asks.

"I think we are close to the North Pole where I live since there is a lot of snow like this near my home with Santa."

"So does that mean we are close?" asks Lucy.

"I am not sure, but I do hope so."

"Whoa! What is that? "The group announces as they come to a fast stop. "I think it is a moose," guesses Lucy. "Let's go see," Jingle Bell says as he tries to be brave, even though he is a little scared too.

The group runs over, a little scared because they do not know what to expect.

"Um Hello?" they shyly say to the moose.

"Hello, young ones. What are you doing all the way up here?"

Jingle Bell speaks up and says, "My name is Jingle Bell and I am Santa's puppy and I really want to go home. Do you think you can help us find him? Have you seen him?"

"Actually I have, I saw him flying over about a week ago."

"THAT WAS CHRISTMAS EVE! The night I got lost," Jingle Bell cries.

"Little Buddy, it's ok, I think I know someone who can help."

Jingle Bell, Lucy and Molly follow the wise moose. They feel like they have been walking for months, but really it has only been about a day. Finally, they stop, seeming to be in the middle of a large snowball when through the snow they spot a black cave.

"Who lives there?" asks Lucy.

"Wait and see," the moose replies back.

Next thing you know they see a bright red light glowing out of the dark cave.

"It's Rudolf," yells Jingle Bell as he runs to him.

"I am home, I am home!" cries Jingle Bell.

"Jingle Bell where have you been?" Rudolf asks.

"I fell out of Santa's bag on Christmas Eve."

"Don't worry you're home now. Let's go find Santa."

The group follows Rudolf's trail. In the distance, you can see the bright lights of the North Pole. When they start to get close, they turn around to see the moose leaving. They want to tell him thank you. Hearing their yelling voices, the moose turns around and gives a big smile with a nod of his head.

North Pole

Jingle Bell, Lucy and Molly go and find Santa-a sight that Molly and Lucy had never seen before. Amazed, they just stand there in shock as Jingle Bell runs to meet Santa once again.

"Jingle Bell, Where have you been? I have been worried about you, but I can see you found some new friends," said Santa.
"I have Santa! They are the best friends any puppy could ever have. They all helped me find you; can they stay here and live with us at the North Pole?" begs Jingle Bell.
"Of course they can."

Molly and Lucy lived happily at the North Pole, along with Jingle Bell and Santa. So just remember anytime you hear a bell jingle, know that Jingle Bell is riding the sleigh with Santa, watching to see if you have been naughty or nice.

Ashley Groves is the author and illustrator of the children's book *Jingle Bell: Santa's Lost Puppy*. Ashley was born in Baltimore, Maryland and resides with her parents (Tracy and Teresa) and younger sister (Lindsey), in Eldersburg, Maryland. Currently Ashley is attending Carroll Community College and is on the Dean's list.

Printed in the United States
By Bookmasters